For Sophie, who showed me the way,
and for Amy, Ashey, and JoJo, for being
our destination. —JL

For Sheila Barry and
Michael Solomon. Thank you for
believing in me. — SS

Groundwood Books / House of Anansi Press
110 Spadina Avenue, Suite 801, Toronto, Ontario M5V 2K4
or c/o Publishers Group West
1700 Fourth Street, Berkeley, CA 94710

We acknowledge for their financial support of our publishing program the Canada Council for the Arts,
the Government of Canada through the Canada Book Fund (CBF) and the Ontario Arts Council.

Canada Council   Conseil des Arts
for the Arts   du Canada

ONTARIO ARTS COUNCIL
CONSEIL DES ARTS DE L'ONTARIO
an Ontario government agency
un organisme du gouvernement de l'Ontario

Library and Archives Canada Cataloguing in Publication
Lawson, JonArno, author
Sidewalk flowers / by JonArno Lawson ; illustrated
by Sydney Smith.
Issued in print and electronic formats.
ISBN 978-1-55498-431-2 (bound).—ISBN 978-1-55498-432-9 (pdf)
I. Smith, Sydney, illustrator II. Title.
PS8573.A93S53 2015   jC813'.54   C2014-905597-8
C2014-905598-6

FSC
www.fsc.org
MIX
Paper from
responsible sources
FSC® C012700

The illustrations were done in pen and ink and watercolor, with digital editing.
Design by Michael Solomon
Printed and bound in Malaysia

Sidewalk Flowers

JonArno Lawson   Sydney Smith

GROUNDWOOD BOOKS
HOUSE OF ANANSI PRESS
TORONTO   BERKELEY

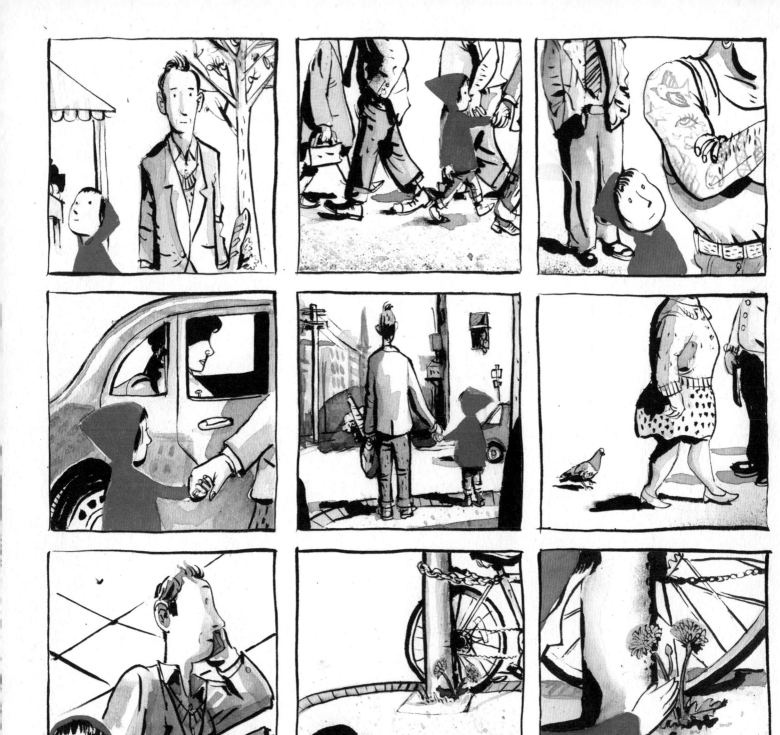